MUSHMOUTH AND THE MARVEL

Mushmouth

and the Marvel

Ted Staunton

Kids Can Press Ltd.
Toronto

Kids Can Press Ltd. acknowledges with appreciation
the assistance of the Canada Council
and the Ontario Arts Council
in the production of this book.

Canadian Cataloguing in Publication Data

Staunton, Ted, 1956–
  Mushmouth and the marvel

ISBN 0-921103-60-3

I. Title.

PS8587.T38M88   1988 jC813'.54 C88-094262-2
PZ7.S72Mu   1988

Printed and bound in Canada by Webcom Ltd.
Cover design by N.R. Jackson
Edited by Charis Wahl
Typeset by Compeer Typographic Services Limited

Kids Can Press Ltd., Toronto

88 0 9 8 7 6 5 4 3

Contents

For Rob, a long way from Etobicoke

Sweet Teeth

Becoming a genius was the dumbest thing I ever did. I'd always wanted to be one, back when I was plain old Cyril, but that was because my friend Maggie, the Greenapple Street Genius, was always bossing me. Maggie moved down to Maple Avenue in December and decided to call herself the Maple Avenue Marvel, and I did a couple of smart things, so I got to be Genius on Greenapple Street. I didn't go bragging or anything, but it felt nice. Maybe Maggie wouldn't be so bossy now. After all, if I was a genius I wouldn't need much help. That's what I thought, anyway. Which is the problem with being a genius: you're not only supposed to think all the time, you're supposed to be right. I was right for two months and nine days, then I was all wrong. Just in time for Valentine's.

All of us in Room 7, Mr. Flynn's class, got invitations to a Valentine party at Karina's house.

It was going to be on Saturday. Everybody got pretty excited when she handed out our invitations on Monday morning. If you didn't count little kid birthdays, nobody had ever had a party for girls and boys before.

"What'll we do there?" I heard George asking Bobby Devlin.

"Games and stuff, maybe dancing," said Bobby, like he'd been to millions of them. He was always showing off. "And if her parents go upstairs I'll teach everybody Spin the Bottle this way my brother told me."

"Bald Potatoes!" I thought. Dancing. Spin the Bottle. It made me half want to giggle and half hope that Karina's parents stuck around.

Then, as Mr. Flynn started arithmetic, we noticed all the invitations were different. Everybody started swapping them around when Mr. Flynn wasn't looking. I'd seen about ten when Lester whispered to me, "Hey, Cyril, see Steve's?"

"No," I hissed back, "but I like Monica's."

Behind me there was this snorting noise from Leanne. I started to turn, but Mr. Flynn was watching us. We all pretended to work until he looked away, then Lester said, "Can't hear ya."

I leaned over to him and saw Leanne whispering to someone else. By spelling time, the whole class was whispering. By reading, they were peeking at me and giggling. By recess, they were saying it out loud: *Cyril said he liked Monica.*

And even worse: Monica said she *loved* me.

It felt like standing in a spotlight and having your pants fall down. The more I yelled that I hadn't said it, the more everybody said, "Suuuuuure, Cyril. When are you getting married?" I ended up roaring that I hated Monica, which wasn't true. Monica was a real motormouth, but I didn't *not* like her. I just didn't want to get married to her, and genius or not I couldn't think of anything else to say.

Maggie didn't tease me, but she wouldn't help either. She said she had to spend all her time keeping an eye on Russell Hummaker. Russell was this new kid who had moved into Maggie's place on Greenapple Street. He was always boasting about how everything was better where he used to live. That bugged Maggie so much she called him a toad. Then she called him a shifty-eyed wolf in sheep's clothing because he was really smart and teachers loved him but he did these hilarious imitations of them when they weren't around. Teachers didn't like Maggie so much; I think she made them nervous. Russell'd just done the best in public speaking and his team was winning noon-time floor hockey. So these days Maggie was calling Russell a slimy rodent. Still, I didn't think Maggie should get that worried. She was Maple Avenue Marvel, after all.

Anyway, I could tell the real reason why she wouldn't help: she thought my problem was one big joke. She had to clamp her lips shut to keep from falling down and howling any time I mentioned Monica.

"But this is so dumb," I moaned to her. "What does Monica love me for? I only sit next to her in reading club."

"You said you liked her, Cyril."

"*I did not*," I roared. "Lizard's Gizzards!"

"Anyway," Maggie snickered, "she thinks you did. And she thinks you're cute. She told us." Us meant the girls.

I made a liver-for-dinner face. How come Maggie always knew more about me than I did?

Maggie grinned this disgusting grin. "All the girls think you're shy. Bonnie's reading this romance book and she says you're 'worshipping from afar'. They think you've been keeping this a big secret."

"*I have not*. You tell them. They'll believe you."

"Uh-uh." Maggie shook her head. "They'd just say I'm jealous because we're partners sometimes, and they wouldn't tell me things. Then we'd both be in trouble."

I sighed. Maggie said, "Hey, you're a genius now. You'll think of something."

When I went home for lunch, my dad was no help either. Ever since Christmas he'd been staying home every day to finish writing a book about businesses. The newspaper that he was a reporter for was letting him do it. At first it seemed really

12

special, but now writing a book just meant a lot of boring talk at dinner when I had real neat stuff to tell. Still, with Dad around, I could come home at lunch even though my mom was school teaching.

So I hemmed and hawed and asked what my dad would do if some girl loved him and everybody thought he loved her.

He said, "Well Cyril, that's what being married is."

I squirmed in my chair. Mushy stuff, especially parent-type mushy stuff, embarrasses me.

Then my dad said, "But for you—"

"It's not me," I said, fast.

"Right," he said. "But it might be tough for a single guy. The best thing is to ignore what people say and pretty soon they'll forget about it. And to try not to hurt the girl's feelings. That would be mean, especially if she really liked a handsome guy like you."

"*HOT TOMATOES, IT'S NOT ME.*"

"Hot tom—" said my dad.

"It's not me," I cut in. I didn't want my dad asking about Hot Tomatoes now. I was in enough trouble.

"Oh," he said, "yes, sorry, I forgot. Tell the guy to ignore it." He gave me some more milk and started bugging me about leaving dirty clothes under my bed on laundry day. Lately he was getting very fussy.

Well, ignore it was easy for my dad to say. He

didn't have to go back to school. There they were chanting:

Cyril and Monica, sitting in a tree,
K-I-S-S-I-N-G,
First comes Love, then comes Marriage,
Then comes Monica with a baby carriage!

Maggie just laughed and kept watching Russell. Monica giggled with a bunch of the girls. I wanted to bury my head in a snow bank, but there wasn't enough snow.

Things got worse and worse. I couldn't line up for anything without getting shoved in next to Monica. Our names got written in the Valentine heart on the bulletin board. When we shared a book in reading club, Monica blushed all over the place and I was so nervous I could hardly read. I started to twitch every time somebody said "Saturday" or "party." I could see Monica plopped in my lap in musical chairs, bonked into me if it was blind man's buff. And what if, because of Valentine's Day, I had to kiss her? In front of people? My stomach heaved and my legs went numb. It would be *so* disgusting, worse than picking someone else's nose.

Then Mr. Flynn announced that our at-school Valentine's party would be skating in the park behind the school on Friday afternoon. Usually I didn't much like skating because I was kind of crummy at it but this time I could hardly even wait.

It was a genius plan, it was mine, and it was simple. All I had to do was show Monica what a klutzy skater I was and she'd forget all about me. That's why, when I wobbled out onto the ice on Friday afternoon all padded up in my snow suit, there was only one thing I wanted to do: fall down.

Believe me, it wasn't hard. I went down on my stomach, my rear, my side, my hands and knees. Around me the good skaters flashed by: Bobby and Lester, George, Karina, Maggie and Russell, stealing hats and mitts, playing tag, going backwards, doing show-off stops that sprayed you. Mr. Flynn glided around like there was nothing to it, little icicles hanging from his moustache. I made sure to trip on my scarf and drag myself around by the boards. It had to be working, I thought. Nobody could be in love with a skater like me. Then this gang of girls grabbed me and stuck me at the end of the line for crack-the-whip, right next to guess who.

"That was great, Cyril."

"Fantastic."

"Cyril's playing he can't skate."

"— ever funny."

They were twittering like a bunch of loony birds. They made us hold hands and my heart sank. Monica just smiled and smiled, not talking for once. I stood there like a goal post. Then the line started moving. Bobby and some others came up behind us singing, "DA DA DA-DA, DA DA DA-DA," the wedding march, until the whip cracked and I slid off into a corner on my rear end. Bobby called, "Hey Cyril, better practise your kissing. Spin the Bottle is just for you!" Then I hit the boards with a thump.

"Frozen Gizzards," I said. The Greenapple Street Genius was in big trouble.

I felt like a total bozo, but I went back to Maggie. I begged and pleaded until she finally said, "Oh, all right. As long as you do everything I say."

It nearly killed me but I said okay. But I did get her to promise she wouldn't tell anyone. This whole thing was already bad enough.

After school we went straight to Maggie's to think. All the way she complained about how Russell cheated at tag and how she was going to get even, but I hardly listened. In my mind I kept seeing a big bottle slowly turning to point at me and Monica, with lips like life preservers.

Maggie's house was half-way along Maple Avenue. You could just see her window from mine, across the back yards and between the houses. It was old I guess, and big. It had to be big because Maggie's mom had had twins and part of the house was an office for Maggie's dad. He was a dentist. If you went in the front door or the back, you got to the house part, but if you went to the side, by the dentist sign, you were in the office.

We clomped through the back door into the

kitchen and dumped our boots and coats and skates. I went to the phone to call home.

"Punch the first button," Maggie reminded. Their telephone had two numbers. The second was only for the office.

I called my dad but I could barely hear him because Maggie's mom came downstairs with a twin bawling its head off and Maggie started complaining about what they were having for dinner and then the other twin started crying somewhere and Maggie's mom had to take off upstairs. When I hung up Maggie said, "Let's go see my dad. Then we'll think."

She led me down the hall to a door that went into the office. We weren't supposed to go in without permission.

"We're not allowed," I warned.

"It's okay," said Maggie, and walked right in.

Mrs. Crumpmeyer, the lady who worked for Maggie's dad, didn't look too pleased to see us.

"Your father's very busy, Maggie," she said. The people in the waiting room stared at us. Maggie stared right back. Just then Maggie's dad stepped out of the room that had his dentist chair, drying his hands on a paper towel. He looked really neat in his blue dentist shirt. My dad wore a lumpy old sweater for writing.

Maggie's dad said, "Mrs. Crumpmeyer, please order some propylene glycol base. We're almost out."

Maggie elbowed me. "Sweet Teeth," she said.

I said, "Huh?" but she was already asking her dad could she mix some up.

"Sure, sure," he said. "But listen, kids, this is not a good time. People are waiting, so I'll see you later, okay?" He leaned through the doorway when we were back in the hall. "And Maggie, we don't just drop in any time, hmm?" Then he was gone.

Maggie scowled for a second, then brightened up. "He sure was busy, huh? It's always like that 'cause he's so good. Wait'll we make Sweet Teeth, though. It's this special formula and I get to make it. See, propylene glycol is really—"

It sounded like it was going to be one of Maggie's long explanations and I wanted her thinking about something else. I said, "I don't care what it is. We're supposed to be thinking about tomorrow."

"Oh, Cyril."

"Well," I said, "aren't we? I bet you forgot already."

Maggie rolled her eyes. And stopped. "Well, as a matter of fact . . ."

"You've got a plan?"

"Maybe," she sniffed. "Almost, anyway. My brain is always working, Cyril. Not like some people's."

I let that go and said, "So what is it?"

"Wait and see."

"Oh, Squashed Tomatoes," I grunted.

"Cyril," she said, "what *is* all this junk about potatoes and lizards and tomatoes you keep saying?"

I felt kind of dumb. I was used to saying those things to myself and I forgot other people could hear.

"I got them from my dad," I explained. "He was talking about this man he went to interview for his book. This guy kept calling stuff Lizard Gizzards and Hot Tomatoes and Bald Potatoes and all this."

"Bald Potatoes?" said Maggie.

"Something like that. It's about business stuff. I just like the way they sound, like swear words, but not really? Especially if you mix them up. But I try not to say them around my dad. He might get mad."

"Right," said Maggie. "Hey, let's play a game."

"But the *plan*," I said.

"I already told you, wait and see."

And that's what I had to do, all the way up to Saturday afternoon at quarter to two when I stamped up Maggie's front steps in the freezing cold. It was time to go to the party. Underneath my snow suit I had on my new corduroys and a clean shirt and socks. My face was washed and my hair combed. I even had a handkerchief in my pocket. But inside I was a mess. Nightmares about what might happen rippled down my stomach like cold caterpillars. Maggie better have a good plan.

The door opened and Maggie came out, making sure not to let the storm door slam. "You shouldn't have knocked so loud," she said. "The twins are napping." Then she banged down the wooden steps to the sidewalk.

We headed down Maple Avenue toward the school, Maggie marching ahead, me dragging behind.

"Why don't you go alone and say I'm sick?" I suggested. "I could wait at your place."

Maggie turned and put her hands on her hips. "No way, Cyril. We're going to take care of this now. Because the Maple Street Marvel has done it again." Out of her pocket she pulled a little bottle of clear, green junk. "A special formula just for you."

I stared. It looked like the dish soap my dad used. "Sweet Teeth," Maggie announced. "Now listen. Monica likes you 'cause you're shy, so you're going to be the opposite and scare her away. With this you're going to be Lance Romance!"

"I can't do it," I said.

"You have to," said Maggie, "or you'll be going on a honeymoon. Now here's what to do. Before Spin the Bottle you sneak in the washroom, swirl Sweet Teeth around in your mouth and spit it out. Make sure you keep your mouth closed and look romantic until kissing time. Then open wide, smile, breathe out heavy and look happy. Monica will probably hide in the garage."

"Stupid Potatoes," I said. "If she thinks I'm romantic, she'll love me more."

"Cyril," Maggie sighed, "all Monica really likes is blabbing and reading horse books. Believe me, it'll work."

We turned up Karina's street and Maggie handed me the bottle. I weighed it suspiciously in my hand. If this mouthwash made me smell good I'd be sunk. Look what happened to people in TV commercials. Then it hit me. I almost laughed out loud. Maggie was tricking me too, just like always. Sweet Teeth was going to make me smell *bad* and scare Monica away. She'd take off for sure, and if she didn't really love me, like Maggie said, she wouldn't be hurt. Maggie had it all figured out, but she forgot she was dealing with another genius.

"Are you sure it'll work?" I whispered, playing along. I tried to smell the bottle. Maybe I could slip some in Maggie's pop. She said, "Nothing happens till it goes in your mouth, Cyril. There's nothing to smell. Now stash it before somebody sees you."

We went up to the house and Maggie rang the bell.

The whole party was sick, gross, disgusting, totally awful and a catastrophe. I never once stopped squirming. Maggie had said to act romantic, but I couldn't do it. I just kept shoving food into my mouth so I wouldn't have to talk, and all

21

the time I could see Bobby waiting for Karina's parents to go upstairs so he could start Spin the Bottle. I got so scared I headed for the washroom early to use my Sweet Teeth.

I shut the door and followed Maggie's instructions, but nothing happened. There was no taste and no smell. A cold sweat broke out over me. What had gone wrong? Someone pounded on the door and I jumped.

Bobby's voice shouted, "Hurry up, Cyril! You fall in or what?"

I clamped my mouth shut and tore out of the bathroom.

"Can't hide in there," Bobby called. I ignored him. I had to get to Maggie, fast.

But Maggie was arm wrestling. I couldn't barge in. As I waited, hopping from foot to foot, I saw Karina's parents heading for the stairs. I was desperate. Cautiously I leaned over to Lester, who was watching the arm wrestling. I breathed out a big sigh. He didn't notice a thing.

That did it. I backed against the wall and inched toward the stairs. With the radio blaring and everybody running around maybe no one would notice till I was gone. I squinched along under the window, looking at the ceiling, the balloons, sliding out my foot to bump that bottom stair. Then I turned, right into Bobby and George.

"C'mon, Cyril," they grinned, "it's that time."

We sat in a circle on the floor, eight of us, with everyone else gathered around to watch. There was a lookout on the stairs. Monica was right across from me. Maggie seemed to have disappeared. Maybe the whole plan had been a joke on me. The Genius gets tricked again. I sighed and looked at the floor. It was cold.

Bobby explained the game. The first time the bottle pointed at you, you had to touch toes; the second, you hooked little fingers; the third, you shook hands; the fourth, you kissed. For a second I felt better. With all those steps maybe I'd never even get to kissing. Then we started and in about ten seconds I was already shaking hands. I was a human magnet for Spin the Bottle. Nobody else had even hooked fingers yet and I was already doomed.

Across the circle, Bobby grinned. He looked like some stupid clown with orange pop all around his mouth.

"This is it," he said. "Somebody's kissing this time." "Kissing" came out like he was slurping an ice cube. Monica reached out to spin the bottle and I got the cold pricklies. I felt like a sick cactus. I knew who was going to be kissing who. Monica was blushing, her eyes like bowls of chocolate pudding. I swallowed hard and tasted my breath: nothing.

She flicked the bottle and I closed my eyes. You could hear it rattle on the floor as it spun, then the noise died away. When I opened my eyes, it was pointing right at me.

There was a cheer. Hands grabbed me and

bundled me across the circle. Monica giggled, trying to keep her lips puckered. I tasted my breath one last time: still nothing. But it was my only chance. I pulled back my lips in the best grin I could manage and wheezed out a big sigh. Monica's jaw nearly hit the floor. She looked as if she'd seen a ghost. Then her mouth twisted up.

"Ewwwwwwwwwwwww," she cried, and burst into tears.

"Whaa?" I said. I looked around. The clutching hands dropped away. Everyone took a step back. I still couldn't smell a thing. Then I heard Maggie say, "We gotta go." Next thing I knew she was dragging me to the stairs.

As we hurried with our boots at the side door, I gasped, "I didn't think it was going to work. I couldn't smell anything."

"Smell?" said Maggie. "Smell? Cyril, you bozo, look in the mirror!" I turned to the hall mirror, grinned, and almost fell downstairs. My whole mouth was a sick, blotchy green.

"Thanks, 'bye," Maggie called up the stairs, then hauled me out the door. I started spitting and slobbering like crazy.

"What did you do me?" I yelled. "I'm dying!"

"You are not," said Maggie. "It's just Sweet Teeth."

"But my mouth is wrecked!"

Maggie sighed. "It's just food colouring, Cyril. It'll come off as soon as you brush your teeth."

"But you said it was Sweet Teeth," I roared. "That's Proppy-something."

Maggie laughed her I'm-smart laugh. "Propylene glycol is the fancy name for the main part of food colouring. My dad calls it Sweet Teeth. He gives it to people who don't brush very often and it makes 'em brush better. See, when you rinse your mouth with it, your teeth turn blotchy everywhere you missed brushing. Since you spent the whole party stuffing your face with pickles and ketchup potato chips, your mouth is extra disgusting." She laughed again.

"Really?" I said.

"Really," said Maggie. "And not only did I get you out of kissing for now, but Monica will never bug you again if she thinks your mouth looks like that. You sure didn't act very romantic, though."

"Aw, come on," I said. "You know I can't do that stuff."

"Skip it," Maggie sighed. "But if anybody asks, say it's a mysterious disease and you never know when it's going to strike. Better yet, keep your mouth shut and—"

"No problem," I said.

"*And*," Maggie went on, "don't forget, you owe me for this. Hey, did you hear I beat Russell the Rodent at arm wrestling?"

She talked about it all the way to Maple Avenue. I didn't mind. Keeping my mouth shut felt just fine.

Snow Good

Keeping my mouth shut at home was easy—my mom was busy planning a volleyball tournament for her school and my dad was thinking about his book and cleaning the basement. But at school it was a lot harder.

As soon as I hit the schoolyard Monday morning, I was surrounded. Everybody was calling out at once.

"Hey, Cyril, show us your mouth!"

"Are you still green?

"You should have seen it, it was all pukey, like."

"And slimy!"

"Oh, gross!"

"Disgusting!"

"Believe it!"

They made me climb up on the jungle gym so they could see.

I was going to say what Maggie told me, about the mysterious disease, but it was such a neat trick and everybody was waiting. I mean, I had to do something. You don't get treated like a big star every day. Before I knew it, "Sweet Teeth" had kind of popped out. Then everybody wanted to know what that was, so I told them, and then they thought it was my idea, so I let on it was, sort of.

Then big mouth Bobby shouted, "He fooled her! Looooook out! Cyril fooled Monica!"

Then everyone was talking at once again, saying, "Totally awesome," and "Radical or what, eh!", and how they'd thought it was a trick. I stood on the jungle gym feeling like the Greenapple Street Genius again, until someone said, "Wait till Monica finds out." Then I didn't feel so good. It was like I'd yelled at a little kid who was bugging me: you know you're not supposed to, but you just have to do it. What if she cried, I thought, climbing down off the bars. Monica was a crier — once when someone gave her ketchup in a peanut butter sandwich it was like the end of the world. If that made her bawl, this would flood the place.

I went into Room 7 and tried to get interested in the hockey cards that George was showing off. Secretly though, I was watching for Monica. I knew the girls would grab her as soon as she came in, and that's what happened. I ducked behind George and clenched my teeth, waiting for the wail.

Instead there was an explosion. Monica practically had steam coming out of her ears. She charged across the room and stuck her nose right in my face.

"You're a big creep, Cyril," she shouted, "and I hate you forever, you . . . MUSHMOUTH."

"Bald Potatoes!" I said, and backed into a desk, I was so surprised.

"Mushed potatoes," Monica sneered back. "You mushed potato Mushmouth. Better watch out, Mushmouth. I'm going to get you for sure." She spun on her heel and marched away as Mr. Flynn came into the room. He didn't notice a thing.

By lunch time my name was Mush, and I was worried.

"You'd better watch out for her, Cyril," Maggie warned. "Better make a plan. I told you to keep quiet."

"But it was your stupid idea," I said.

"I'm the brains, Cyril, not the mouth. And you made me promise not to tell, didn't you? Hmmm?"

"Mouthy Tomatoes," I sighed.

For the next two days I kept my back to the wall, any wall. That way nobody could sneak up. Monica and the girls stayed away from me, but I didn't like the way they huddled over by the basketball hoop all the time, watching. I asked Maggie what was up but she didn't know. Or care. She was too busy with these puzzle books to find out. Maggie was steamed because Mr. Flynn had read us these one-minute mysteries in class and Russell had solved three of them while Maggie only got one. I didn't get any. Mr. Flynn said Russell was a great detective. Maggie snorted that he was a Great Defective and that he must have cheated, and now they were at war. Mr. Flynn had promised to read some more mysteries at the end of the week so Maggie was boning up like crazy.

Which is why she was standing against the wall beside me at Wednesday recess, her nose in a book, when Russell and Bobby came up, grinning.

"Hi Mush," said Bobby. "Hi Muggy. Watcha doin', holdin' the wall up?"

"Go suck eggs, Booby," said Maggie without looking up.

Then Russell said, "Hey Maggie, did you hear? There's a snow storm coming." Something sly in the way he said it made Maggie look up.

"So," she said, "who cares?" but she watched him like a hawk. Well I cared, for one. It had been a dull winter for snow. We'd only had a teeny bit and I liked a ton of it.

Russell said, "Back at our old place it always snowed way more than this."

"It hasn't snowed any more across town either, Russell," Maggie said flatly. "So what's the big deal?"

Russell shrugged. "Nothing. I just want to go snow shovelling, make some money for a special project."

"Like what?" Maggie made a bored face.

Russell smiled till his eyes almost disappeared.

"Like a tree-house kit from the lumber company. When spring comes, me and my brother are going to tear down that piece of junk you built and make a *real* tree house."

Maggie shot off the wall like a bullet. Bobby jumped back, but Russell didn't, which was amazing. The look Maggie was giving him, he should have fried up into a little pile of ashes.

"That's *my* tree house," she breathed, and it sounded scary. Everybody knew that tree house was Maggie's favourite place in the whole world. It was where she used to hide stuff and make plans and spy and you could only go in if she invited you. She even wanted to take it with her when she moved, but there was no place for it in her new back yard.

"Don't touch it," she said. "Don't you even try, Russell."

"Make me," he said.

" I don't make monkeys," Maggie snapped back.

"Oh yeah?" said Russell. "I bet you looked like one in that garbage tree house." Bobby nearly split a gut at that one. Russell turned to go. "I just hope they pay good on Crabapple Street. I don't want to go out more than once or twice."

"It's Greenapple," I shouted as he walked away, "and they pay great!" They didn't pay that great, but he wasn't cutting up my street and getting away with it.

"Greenapple, Crabapple," said Russell. "They sure have stupid street names around here." And he strolled off with Bobby like he was king of the world.

Maggie watched them go. Her face was white and you could see her teeth grinding. Even I'd never seen her so mad before. "I'm going to stop him, Cyril. That little tree toad can't do this to me."

"What are you going to do?"

"I don't know yet." She slapped her book against her leg. "But till I do we've got to stall him. You owe me for Sweet Teeth, Cyril, so when it snows we're going to shovel Greenapple Street first, like always, and get the money he needs. It's our street, right?"

"Right," I sighed. I had been thinking about tobogganing.

"We'll clean his clock," Maggie said. She was cheering up already.

"Frozen Gizzards," I said. I kept my back against the wall for the rest of recess and wondered why I couldn't make plans for Monica as fast as Maggie did for Russell.

The snow began the next morning, big fat flakes in the grey sky. By recess it was falling thick and heavy and by lunch time the wind had picked up and ice pellets stung our faces. "Be ready after school," Maggie warned me. "We'll have to move fast."

"What if he's already asked everybody if he can do their snow?"

"He hasn't," said Maggie. "He was bragging to me he didn't need to."

The snow scratched and rattled at the windows nearly all afternoon. It made Room 7 feel pretty cozy, for school. Russell kept looking at Maggie and grinning. Maggie acted like nothing was wrong. Monica kept peeking at some book in her desk. I stared out the window and did some thinking. It seemed to me that if I did something mean to Monica it would just make her madder, so I had to make her not mad before she did something mean to me. I could say I was sorry but keep my fingers crossed, because I wasn't sorry since she'd yelled at me. She'd suspect something, though. But maybe if I gave her something, not mushy but okay, maybe then she'd believe me. Something like, say, hockey cards. Then I remembered these neat mini-jigsaw puzzles they had at the variety store. And after we went snow shovelling I'd have enough money for sure. I sat up straight and checked the clock. Snow shovelling was suddenly a big deal.

Right around three o'clock the storm died out. Maggie gave me the signal and when the bell rang, we were jamming on our boots before Russell even had his chair on his desk.

"How come he wasn't rushing?" I called as we burst out the doors.

"That's his problem," Maggie called back. "Ten minutes. We start at Elston's like usual." Then she was gone.

I shot home like I was on rocket skis, jumped over my dad who was washing the kitchen floor, yelled where I was going and grabbed a cookie. My dad got kind of mad because I'd tracked all over the wet floor. "Soapy Potatoes," I muttered, then yelled "Sorry," as I ran out the door. My dad said cleaning was better than sitting when he got stuck on his book, but I didn't figure he was stuck enough to like the snow I left in the hall.

Outside it was getting colder. A last few snow-flakes were wobbling down as I grabbed our snow shovel and set off up Greenapple Street. Maggie was already clearing the steps at Elston's when I got there. There was no sign of Russell.

I dug in and we shovelled like crazy. The snow was powdery light except at the street, where the snowplough had pushed up a slush wall. We raced through the walk and driveway but when we hit the slush, we bogged down. Boy, was it heavy. It stuck to your shovel like glue, too. After a minute I stopped to get my breath. My scarf was all soggy from my breath steaming out and my ears were hot and itchy.

"Maybe Russell chickened out," I said. I lifted my hat and the cold rushed at my head.

"Uh-uh," Maggie said. She never stopped shovelling. "Something must be going on. We'd better hurry."

But I didn't want to hurry, not yet anyway. Everything was white and rounded over with snow and it was so still you could hear the quiet pinging all around. I listened hard. Way far away a car was spinning its wheels, the snowplough was chugging, then THWUCK, Maggie's shovel scraped the driveway. "Come *on*, Cyril," she said, and I went back to work.

THWUCK. We shovelled hard into the slush and heaved. *Fwump*, it landed. It was freezing up fast. THWUCK, we shovelled again. *Fwump*. THWUCK. THWUCK.

Then another noise floated up Greenapple Street, a REEEEEEEE like an electric lawn mower. Except it wasn't a lawn mower, it was Russell and his brother cleaning Pederson's driveway with a little snow thrower. We stopped and stared as the snow sprayed out like Niagara Falls. Russell pushed it and his brother cleaned up behind with a shovel. Russell blew away the slush at the end of Pederson's drive like dust. I felt like slush myself.

"Bald Lizards," I said. "No wonder he didn't hurry. They'll clean us."

"We've gotta try," said Maggie. "C'mon."

It wasn't much of a race. They whisked from house to house while we slogged along, falling further and further behind. "Maybe it'll break down," I said as we worked at Vulkovich's. Maggie kept shovelling. Then she stopped and grinned. "Or maybe," she said, "they'll get stuck at Old Man Billings'." I had to grin, too.

Old Man Billings lived half-way down

Greenapple Street. He'd stand at the window watching and if he caught you for snow shovelling you were dead. His driveway went way back of the house. It was gravel and the snow was always lumpy from the stones underneath. A driveway like that would take forever to clear, even with a snow thrower. Even worse, Old Man Billings paid so crummy that it was like not getting paid at all. My parents said he meant well. I thought he meant cheap.

Now Russell and his brother were right next door to Billings'. We were five houses away, shovelling beside a hedge. The noise of the snow thrower stopped. We peeked over the bushes and saw Russell and his brother laughing and talking as they got their money.

"They're doomed." Maggie said it like an evil genius in a horror movie.

They started down the steps. Any second now Old Man Billings would open his door and call for them in his scratchy voice.

"Here it comes," said Maggie. Up we went on tiptoe, holding our breath, and a scratchy voice behind us said, "Say there, you two. You come over and do my place next, now." We whirled around to see Old Man Billings in his boots and big old overcoat, with a bag of groceries in his hand. We were doomed.

A million years later we were still digging away at Billings' driveway when Russell and his brother walked by on their way home. They'd done almost the whole street.

Russell called over, "Hey Mush, what's taking so long?"

Maggie turned her back and shovelled harder. I looked at him and wished a tree would fall on his head. My toes were frozen, my back was sore, my fingers were stuck to my shovel like claws, my snow suit weighed a ton, and it felt like there was an icicle hanging from my nose. Plus, I was starving. "Guess you wish you got the biggest job on the street, huh?" It was the only thing I could think of that was even half-way smart.

Russell patted the snow thrower. "Don't worry," he said. "Next time." Then he called, "Hey Maggie, one more snow storm and bye-bye tree house!" He went off with his brother, laughing like a hyena. Maggie didn't even turn around.

The street lights had been on a long time when we got done. Maggie took her half of the money and headed for home, the long way, by the street. That meant she was feeling bad. When she was happy she always cut through the back yards. I felt a little bit better. I had enough money for the puzzle and after I begged all through dinner, my mom took me to the variety store that night. My plan was still working.

By the time I got to the school yard the next morning, I was as ready as I'd ever be. I had the puzzle in a plastic bag from the store. It had taken a long time to pick the right one. They'd had a fantastic one of outer-space aliens but I knew Monica would hate that, and a yucky one with little kittens in bows that she'd probably have loved, but it was so disgusting, I got this one of a pizza instead. Now I was going to say sorry with my fingers crossed in my mitts, then give her the puzzle. The only thing was, I didn't want to do it in front of everybody. I had to catch Monica alone.

I spotted her with a bunch of the girls over by one of the basketball poles, so I waited by the corner of the school to see if they'd break up.

"Come on, come on," I muttered, then wished they'd stick together so I wouldn't have to say anything. But then they were looking my way and then Monica was walking over. It was too perfect.

I practised what I was going to say again, fast, under my breath, then leaned back against the wall. My legs had just turned to peanut butter. What if she didn't want to listen? What if she was going to challenge me to a duel or something?

Monica got closer. "Hi, Cyril." She smiled. Bald Potatoes, I thought, she didn't even call me Mushmouth. Maybe she wasn't mad any more. Maybe she couldn't think of a plan. Maybe she got scared of what I might do to her. Maybe this was going to be easier than I thought. I crossed my fingers in my mitts and said, very fast, "Hi, Monica. Sorry I made you cry when my mouth was green."

"That's okay," she said, also very fast. "Sorry

I called you Mushmouth." She put her hands behind her back.

I gave her the pizza puzzle and told her what it was. She said thank you but didn't open the bag. Instead she said, "Will you help me?"

I almost fell into a snow bank. Monica said shyly, "You're good at tricks and things, right, and I want to prove something to the girls. We made a bet."

"You want to play a trick on somebody?" I asked cautiously.

"Yes, but I need your help or they won't believe me."

I let out my breath. She couldn't trick me and need my help at the same time. If I helped we'd be friends again for sure, and that would mean no more Mushmouth. Maybe I'd even get to do the puzzle. I said, "Sure."

Monica led me over to the girls by the basketball pole.

"See," she said, "we have this bet that you can tie somebody up to this pole without rope or anything. But it has to be a boy because it was in this book for boys."

I reached out and patted the pole. It was smooth under my mitten; there was no way you could get caught on it. I looked at Monica. She gave me a big wink. "Okay," I said, "but hurry. The bell's going to ring soon."

In a flash they'd grabbed me and stood me with

my nose to the pole. Then they pulled my feet forward on either side. I had to grab the pole up high to keep from falling down. Next they crossed my right leg over my left and pulled back my right foot and hooked it behind the bottom of the pole. Then Monica pushed me down by the shoulders till I was squatting half-way down, my hands grabbing at the slippery pole above my head. I could feel how cold it was right through my mitts.

"Now," she ordered. "Try to get up."

I huffed and puffed and wriggled and pulled, but I was stuck like glue. My arms were beginning to get tired.

"Wow," I said nervously, "this works great. The girls were right."

"No, I was right," said Monica as the bell rang. "*They* didn't think I could trick you." The girls all giggled.

I stared at her.

"Thanks for helping, Cyril. 'Bye." They all walked away. The giggling turned to laughter.

"Hey," I shouted, "let me up." My arms were killing me now. The girls kept walking.

"Very funny," I called. "Ha ha. Come on, hurry up."

Monica turned around.

"You can stay there forever for all I care, Mushmouth. And you can play with this while you're at it." She threw the puzzle into the snow. "I'm good at tricks too. Now we're even. *And* I had my fingers crossed when I said sorry, 'cause I'm not. So bye-bye, MUSHED POTATOES." They all ran off before I could shout that my fingers were crossed, too.

I yanked at the pole and yelled every name I could think of. If that was the way Monica wanted it, okay. I'd show her, boy. Was she ever going to be sorry. I'd get her really good this time, as soon as I got unwrapped from the pole.

The problem was I couldn't get unwrapped from the pole until Maggie came along and lifted me up as the last kids were going inside. She must have still been feeling bad because she didn't even ask what I was doing wrapped around the basketball pole. I didn't bother to tell her, either.

We slid into our seats in Room 7 as Mr. Flynn was taking attendance. Some of the girls giggled but everyone else ignored us. That was fine with me.

I stared down at my desk. Partly I felt stupid and partly I felt mad that I had to feel stupid. And a teeny tiny little part way down inside felt like maybe I should never have tricked Monica with Sweet Teeth in the first place and maybe now we *were* even. If we weren't, we were at war forever and I didn't want that. I just wasn't like Maggie, always making up plans and tricking people and loving it. I couldn't do it. Then I had a thought I'd never had before: maybe I wasn't *supposed* to be like Maggie. The thought made me feel so strange

I didn't know what to think next. I looked around the room instead, and noticed something new on the bulletin board, something everyone else was already looking at.

It was a poster of the Earth from outer space with the words *A world of problems. A world of knowledge. A world of fun. Are you ready for the challenge?* CHALLENGERSSSSSSSSSSS! Then Mr. Flynn brushed up his moustache, tugged his beard and began to speak. Our class was going to take part in a new TV quiz show for schools called "Challengers." We were all going to go and see the show made, but he was going to pick four of us to be a team and be on TV.

Everybody started talking at once. I was still so mixed up I didn't understand it all, but I got this little shock inside. Even I was beginning to get excited.

Mr. Flynn got us quiet and told the rest. Everybody had a chance for the team. We'd do a TV project in class and take turns playing games and videotaping and doing all the other stuff you'd need for a show and Mr. Flynn was going to watch how we worked. Whoever worked the hardest, thought the quickest and got along with everybody best would get picked, and he'd tell us ten days before the show.

"They tell me that maybe 75,000 people will watch the show," said Mr. Flynn. Then he smiled. "Are you ready for the challenge?"

Right then I knew. I was ready. I could quit being a mushmouth. I could stop fighting with Monica. I could tell about Challengers at dinner and no one would talk about books and volleyball. All I had to do was get on that team.

But could I do it? What was I really, a mushmouth or a genius? Everybody looked so smart all of a sudden. The excitement started to go out of me. Then there was a voice at my ear.

"This is going to be great, Cyril. Wait'll we get on that show. We'll clean up."

I whipped around and there was Maggie.

"Partners?" I cried.

"Smart Potatoes," she said. "What else?"

The Nose That Knows

"Do you think we'll be famous after we get on TV?" Maggie and I were sitting in my kitchen eating cookies. It was past five o'clock but we were allowed, dinner was so late at our places. Maggie's mom had to feed the babies before supper and her dad worked almost till then. My mom was staying late at school for volleyball and my dad was really busy because he had to take some more of his book to the publishing company the next day. Nothing was even thawed for dinner yet. That was good because when he forgot we got pizza sometimes, and I was hoping. Even better was that he wasn't bugging me so much about being neat and tidy. On the other hand, he didn't have time to take us swimming, either, or do the laundry. My socks were getting kind of stinky.

Maggie thought about my question. "We probably won't be *famous* famous. Unless we win and keep going on."

"That would be really great, huh?"

Maggie nodded, her mouth full of cookie. "It's a good thing it's a TV show for geniuses," she said. For two weeks, ever since Mr. Flynn's announcement, we'd been talking about Challengers—that and the tree house. Nobody teased me much about Monica any more, even though they still called me Mushmouth. Room 7 was all giggling about Russell telling the world he beat Maggie at snow shovelling and that she was sucky about her tree house. Some kids were saying maybe Maggie wasn't so smart compared to Russell. Maggie called Bobby a banana brain for that and said Russell better watch out. Mr. Flynn told *her* to watch out. He liked Russell. Russell never got in trouble.

That was when Maggie got very interested in getting me on TV. Everybody knew she was going to get on for sure—as long as she didn't massacre Russell first and get in trouble. But for me it wasn't that easy. For a week the class had been taking turns being the audience, doing music, keeping score, making up questions, running the video camera we borrowed, or best of all, hosting a show or playing. Mr. Flynn was watching all the time. I got to be on the team twice but both times somebody else hogged the show. First it was Russell, who answered nearly every question, and then Bobby kept being funny while he was host. Everybody laughed so much that probably not even Mr. Flynn noticed I got the most right answers. I did my best at all the other work but someone always did better. And I tried to get along with everyone too, but nobody said I was their favourite.

I had one chance left. Tomorrow I was going to host the last game and Maggie was running the camera. Right now we were practising, which was making me wonder. Usually I had to practically cry for her to help, but this time Maggie insisted. First she said it was because we were partners. Then she said it was a secret. Finally she said, "There's only four places on the team, Cyril. If we get two of them, that only leaves two places for everyone else, including Russell, and there's lots of others who're good: Bobby, Monica—"

"Monica!"

"She's excellent at making up questions," Maggie said. "Anyway, even if Russell does get on, we'll never give him a chance to open his mouth. That'll teach the little rodent. Now, let's get busy."

I rolled my eyes. "We've done it fifteen times!"

"Hey," said Maggie, "I'm doing this for us, you know, not just me."

"You just don't want to go home and have to change diapers," I said. Maggie hated that stuff. The twins had diaper rash or something and they were always bawling.

"Cyruullllll," Maggie said, "let's go." She

picked up the camera — really a shoe box with holes in it. I dumped my cookie crumbs onto the floor.

"Ready," she said, "go." I opened my mouth.

"Wait!" she cried. "I can't see you."

"You're looking through the wrong end."

"Oh yeah." She turned the box so that the big hole pointed at me. "You looked better the other way."

I stuck out my tongue.

"Try again," said Maggie. "Ready . . . go."

"Good morning and welcome to 'Challengers'. Today we—"

"Afternoon," said Maggie. "You say 'Good afternoon', remember? Right. Okay, go."

"Good afternoon, everybody and welcome to — to—"

" 'Challengers'," Maggie said.

" 'Challengers'."

"Cyril," called my dad, "keep it down in there, please?"

"SORRY. Okay. Ready, go. Good afternoon and welcome to 'Challengers'. This morning we—"

"No," said Maggie.

"Crummy Lizards," I said.

"CYRIL," called my dad.

"SORRY." I jumped.

"You dummy," Maggie whispered, "he heard you. You're in trouble."

"He probably wasn't paying attention," I said. "He's writing."

It didn't get any better. I got more and more nervous until Maggie got mad and quit. "I'll have to think of something," she said, when she finally left. That didn't help either. I was half angry and half nervous all night long.

Next morning I was scared stiff as peanut brittle.

Room 7 made me feel even weirder. Everything was moved to make a big space in front of Mr. Flynn's desk. Four of our desks faced in on each side like a V and past them stood the video camera. As I sat down at Mr. Flynn's desk, it seemed to be pointed straight at me. Like a gun. I looked down, fast.

In front of me was a paper with what I had to say, a stack of question cards and a pencil. I wished there was a wall instead.

The two teams sat down at the desks. Scorekeepers came to the chalkboard behind me where the "Challengers" poster had been taped up. Everybody else sat back by the coat racks, except Lester, who was running the tape recorder, and Karina, who had to do a commercial. Maggie gave me a long stare, then bent over the camera. It looked a lot meaner than the shoe box.

"All set?" called Mr. Flynn. "Here we go. Five, four, three . . . " He flashed out the countdown with his fingers.

I squirmed one last time. My chair had a phone book on it to boost me higher at the desk and my feet didn't touch the floor. It was hard to keep from sliding around.

" . . . two, one," called Mr. Flynn. He pointed at Lester, who flipped on the tape recorder. The music blared, Maggie swivelled the camera, and everybody in the audience clapped. Then it all died down. I looked up, took a deep breath, and started talking.

The first part went okay, but that camera was like a deep dark hole that had a bear in it. I kept wishing it would smile.

The camera made me so nervous I didn't have a clue who was winning the game. I did notice Monica though. You couldn't help it. She was so fast putting up her hand that I had to keep picking her. As we came to the end of the first half, she just barely beat George to a twenty-point question and she got the right answer, too. George got mad.

After that we stopped while Karina did a cat food commercial. Bobby played the cat. Everybody was laughing but I was still worrying too hard to pay much attention. I'd messed up twice, once when I read an answer instead of a question and once, really bad, when I slid off the phone book and nearly disappeared under the desk. I took a deep breath and sagged on the phone book. The camera was still pointed at Bobby as he pretended to gobble down cat food. Look at Bobby, I told myself. He can do it. Why can't I be like that? I knew I couldn't though, not in a million years, not unless something totally weird happened.

It happened.

I got an itch in my nose.

Not an itch where I could scratch it, but way up inside. Twitching didn't help, neither did sniffing. I couldn't stick my finger up there with everybody watching. It felt like I'd need a hockey stick to reach it, anyway.

Nobody could tell yet, but the itch was getting worse every second, and I was scared stiff. Soon, I knew, I was going to make some horrible mistake and blow my chance to get on TV. I had to hang on. My sweaty hands skidded across the top of the desk. My nose felt like a rocket about to take off.

Then I noticed the pencil. My heart was whumping like a fist in a baseball glove. Somehow I read the next question.

As the answer came back I lifted the pencil to my chin. All I could feel was itch. I was one big nose. I read the next question. A hand went up, the eyes turned away, a voice talked—and behind my hand I plunged the eraser end of the pencil deep into my nose.

It felt so fantastic I nearly laughed out loud. I rubbed the pencil in farther, wanting to go on and on, but the answer was almost done. I whipped out the pencil and grabbed the next question. Then I noticed something strange: the eraser had disappeared. And I felt . . . stuffy, like. Then there was a feeling like snow down my back. I sat up so straight I almost broke my neck. My nose twitched hard. It couldn't be. *Could it?* But as the camera swung back I knew it was. The eraser had stuck in my nose.

"Dad's ride," I said, trying not to moan and hoping the answer was right. "Dow, duh negs quedgon ib . . . " The players were looking at me strangely already. My face began to burn. I rushed on, " . . . negs quedgon ib where duhs duh dame humburgah cumb fwom?"

By the time the show was over everybody except Mr. Flynn was staring and whispering as if I was crazy. I was a wreck. I figured the show was a wreck, too, since all Maggie would have taped was somebody sliding around on a phone book, making faces, and bouncing up and down trying to sneeze and talking like he has a grapefruit up his nose. I wanted to crawl into the bottom drawer of the desk and stay there for a thousand years.

But I had to explain to Mr. Flynn. Then I had to stand there when he blurted, "*ERASER UP YOUR—*" really loud and the whole class found out. I had to let the principal look up my nose with a flashlight in the Home Ec. room and wait while he got out this long pair of tweezers. And when I got back to class with an empty nose I had to pretend not to notice all the whispers and laughing. So I never got to hide in the desk. All I could do was take off as fast as I could when the noon bell rang. Maggie called after me but I didn't care.

When I got half way up Greenapple Street, I stopped and kicked a snowbank to smithereens.

Everything was messed up, *AGAIN, AGAIN, AGAIN*, and we would all watch it *AGAIN* this afternoon. The only time I'd be on TV, ever. I wasn't going to be a star, I was going to be . . . to be . . . A RUBBERNOSE MUSHMOUTH. I knew it, for sure. It wasn't *fair*. I kicked a bigger snowbank to the moon, and another one to Mars. When there was nothing left to kick, I headed for home. My eyes had gone all watery from the cold.

I didn't have to say anything at lunch. My dad was in a hurry to get to his meeting at the publishing company, so he didn't have time to talk much, or even do the dishes. He just checked his briefcase about fifty-three times, plugged in the slow cooker, then we were barrelling out the front door. Next thing I knew he was driving off one way and I was walking the other, heading back to school. It felt like the shortest lunch in history.

I ploughed through all the snow I could find to make the trip last longer. I figured I could wait a long time for what was coming. First there'd be the teasing. Then we'd see the tape and everybody would get a big laugh. At recess the rest of the school would hear what a moron I was and it would be Rubbernose Mushmouth time.

When I got to school, though, there was no teasing. A couple of kids laughed, but some said it was too bad. Monica didn't even call me Mushmouth. Maybe that was because I'd picked her instead of George. I guess everyone thought they could be nice to me now because they knew I'd never be on TV. Besides, we still had to watch the tape.

Maggie didn't show up almost until the bell. That was okay with me, because I figured she was going to kill me for blowing it. But when she raced up all she said was, "Lunch wasn't ready. Guess who mom was busy with?" It wasn't till we were almost at Room 7 that she whispered, "Keep your fingers crossed, Cyril. Hope it works." Before I could ask, "What works?" she was gone.

The TV sat on this tall stand at the front of the room. It looked like the head of an alien. My stomach started doing funny elevator rides.

Mr. Flynn turned off the lights and moved to the TV. "I think you'll find this tape interesting," he said. Interesting! I buried my face in my hands and peeked out between my fingers.

The tape started okay. My voice kept going too soft, but everybody had done that. Then came the part where I read the answer instead of the question. I'd made a stupid face and whispered, "Bald Potatoes!" I held my breath as it came up. Luckily, Maggie had forgotten to turn the camera away from George, so instead of me goofing up all we saw was George listening. I felt better, until I remembered that I fell off the phone book next. But Maggie had blown it again and we didn't see that either. Instead there was a shot of the scoreboard.

Everyone laughed during the commercial. The camera looked right at me as the game started again and I did the twitch. It looked as if I was trying to stick my nose in my ear. There was lots of laughing as the camera jerked back and showed everybody from a long way off. I was glad. You couldn't see me bouncing up and down so much from there. Still, I wanted to shrivel up and disappear, but instead I couldn't help watching.

But odd things were happening. I seemed to have disappeared from the show. My voice was still there, a little fuzzy, but the rest of me had gone to Pluto or somewhere. It was weird. Maggie had really blown it. No wonder she wasn't mad at *me*.

The tape ended looking at the "Challengers" poster as my voice said "gudbuh," for goodbye.

"Terrific," Mr. Flynn said. I nearly fell off my chair.

Mr. Flynn perched on his desk. He was brushing up his moustache like mad.

"That was great team work. You had a little problem there, Cyril." There was giggling until Mr. Flynn said, "Super effort. I don't know if I could have finished the show with an eraser up *my* nose."

"It'd have to be a pretty big eraser," called Bobby. Even I laughed at that. Then I swallowed hard. Mr. Flynn stroked his beard and went on,

"Good work from the players, too. You were all calm and cool enough to pretend there was nothing wrong." That wasn't exactly true, I thought, remembering some funny looks I'd gotten, but I was feeling better enough to let it go.

" . . . and the audience didn't fuss either," Mr. Flynn was saying. I glanced quickly around. Everybody was looking pleased with themselves, except Maggie. She looked nervous.

"Now," said Mr. Flynn. "Here's a question for you: What made this tape so strange?" Everybody talked at once.

"Because Cyril was jumping."

"He talked funny."

"The score was low."

Russell just raised his hand and waited, like always.

"Whoa!" called Mr. Flynn. "Besides those. Russell?"

Loud and clear in his know-it-all voice, Russell said, "Because the camera was all messed up. You couldn't even see who was talking half the time." He shook his head like he was from Hollywood.

"Bingo," said Mr. Flynn. Russell looked like a dog being patted on the head. "And that," said Mr. Flynn, "is what I loved about this tape." I looked fast at Maggie: now *she* looked like the Hollywood expert. Russell looked like somebody had just pulled his tail. The rest of us looked confused.

"This," said Mr. Flynn, "was the first time when the camera wasn't staring in the same place all the time. It was moving, and that made things a lot more exciting. Some of it was pretty rough, and there might have been some accidents, but we're learning here. We didn't see our host in trouble because the camera didn't let us. Maybe the camera operator didn't want us to."

I stared at Maggie. She raised her eyebrows and gave me her I-told-you smile. It was unbelievable.

"Remember that," said Mr. Flynn, and he slapped his desk, "in TV the real star is behind the camera, not in front of it." He stood up and tugged at his beard. "Which brings me to the announcement you've been waiting for." Everybody froze.

"You know I wish I could pick everybody, but I can't. We'll all go the TV studio to watch, so nobody should feel left out. The team members are Maggie, Russell, Monica, and Cyril."

We floated out of school that afternoon, Maggie and me. It all made sense now. I *had* done a good job, I *had* tried hard. No wonder nobody had teased me. Maybe I was the only person who could have done all the stuff I did.

Maggie said, "Well, I did it after all. But, I don't think Mr. Flynn had to say some of it was rough like that. And with you and me and blabbermouth Monica on the team, Russell doesn't stand a chance." She looked at me. "You did okay, too, Cyril."

Okay? No matter what Mr. Flynn said about stars behind the camera, I'd done better than okay. No way was I letting Maggie grab all the glory on this one. I said, "Well, you did *okay*, too. I mean, you could have showed me a little more so it wasn't like I'd died. But having to change your plans—"

"Change my plans?" said Maggie.

"From making me look good to not showing me much," I said.

"Cyril," said Maggie. "Remember when I got the shoe box backwards yesterday and I said you looked better that way? Well, that gave me the idea."

"No way," I said, but I was getting my old sinking feeling. "You didn't even have a plan this morning. You ran the camera like the shoe box. Mr. Flynn even said there were accidents."

"He said they *might* have been accidents," Maggie shook her head.

"You mean you planned it all?" My voice went way up.

"Well," she said, "not the first couple. But when I heard giggling I figured I'd just missed you goofing up. Then I remembered the shoe box and thought what if I didn't show you? So I didn't, and you should be glad."

I looked at her and didn't feel glad at all. I felt tricked again, just like the old days.

"It was not all a plan," I said, just to try one more time. My brains were all jumbled up.

Maggie just smiled and kept walking.

"Star's behind the camera," she said.

"You messed up too," I said.

"You can thank me later," she said, and kept walking.

I had to stop. I was scared I'd fall over. Then Maggie turned around and grinned.

"C'mon Cyril, let's go home and *tell*."

I ran to catch up and all at once I was laughing. Naw, she hadn't fooled me. Well, not really.

Baby Farmers

By the time we hit Maple Avenue we were bursting with our news about TV. We bounced off the snowbanks, swung around trees and chased each other all over the place. We laughed and yelled, and showed each other how our parents would fall over when they heard the news. Then we shouted just to hear the noise. If Old Man Billings himself had popped out of a snow drift, we'd have grabbed him and danced.

We tramped into Maggie's kitchen all giggly and out of breath. "Here goes," said Maggie. "Mom," she called, "Maaa-om!" There was no answer. Then we spotted the note on the table. Maggie's mom had taken the twins for their doctor's checkup and we were supposed to let Maggie's dad know when we got in. We dumped our stuff and raced for the office.

But the waiting room was full of patients and nobody looked too thrilled to see us. Mrs. Crumpmeyer gave us a smile that lasted about one microsecond. She said she'd tell Maggie's dad that we were home, then marched us to the door. She closed it pretty hard, too.

Maggie's face went red and she glared back at the door.

"You can tell them at dinner," I said, to make her feel better.

Just wait till *my* parents got home, I thought.

After a long time Maggie said, "Right," and we ended up playing checkers. The red didn't go out of her face till she beat me.

Well, my parents got home. They said wow, and wonderful, gee, terrific, and isn't that great. But it didn't feel good at all. My dad was mad at his publishers because they didn't like what he wrote and my mom had all these tests to mark. Before you knew it we were back to books and volleyball. I couldn't believe it. When I was a little kid, they'd drool if I brought home a silly finger painting. Now they'd probably yawn if I told them I'd been elected king.

"How come writing a book is so hard if you can write for the newspaper every day?" I asked, poking at a lump of potato with my fork, trying to race it through the gravy and around the rim like a speedboat. It was stew for dinner. I hate stew.

"I don't know, Cyril," my dad sighed, "but it is. The publishers want me to change things around to make it more interesting. The problem is, I can't figure out how."

"Can't they tell you?" I asked. He made a face

like he'd just seen the disgusting piece of meat I was trying to hide in my carrots.

"They're not sure either. We agreed the book would be about businesses people start, right? So each chapter is about a different kind of business. That's what we all decided a long time ago. What else can I do?" He shrugged and mushed some potato around on *his* plate. Then he looked at me and said, "Have you got any ideas, Cyril?"

"I guess not," I said. I wished I did though, because it made me feel grown up to get asked. I tried to make my dad feel better anyway. "Even if it's hard, when you're done and everybody reads your book, you'll be famous. Will we be rich, too?"

He laughed. "I figure I might earn about half of what I might make in a year at the newspaper, so it'll be a long while before we're rich. And as for famous, probably a lot more people will see you on TV than will ever read my book." He shrugged. "Thanks anyway, Cyril."

Not rich! Not famous! I was so amazed I blurted out, "Hot Tomatoes," right there at the table. My dad's head snapped up, but he didn't say anything. My mom said, "Tomatoes, shmomatoes. Tackle those carrots, buster. We don't want you wasting away to nothing and being invisible on TV."

"Awwwww."

"Stars eat stew, too," said my mom. I didn't say it, but I bet they don't.

Use your library

American Library Association

For the next two days my mom stayed late at school. My dad stared at his work and house-cleaned and got grouchy: pick this up, put that away, hang up my coat, wipe my boots, watch the crumbs, turn down the stereo. When I told my mom, all she said was to go easy on my dad. *He* was having a tough time! All I could do was steam around muttering, "Grubby Potatoes" and "Splattered Tomatoes" while I worked like a slave.

Okay, I thought, so writing a book is tough. So volleyball tournaments and marking tests are tough (not as tough as writing them, though). But here I was, the Greenapple Street Genius, going to be more famous than my dad and *I* had to go back and hang up the bath towel and put ency-clopaedias away. I thought they'd want me clean. I thought they'd want me smart. It just wasn't fair.

At school it was different. I wasn't getting called Mushmouth any more. Now it was "Hi Mush," but friendly, like a nickname I'd always had and no one remembered why. Now it was special nice, not special stupid. Only Bobby still said it like he meant it, but he was mad because he didn't get picked for TV, and he made fun of everybody. Except Russell, that is.

Monica just called me Cyril. We weren't best friends or anything, but we weren't at war any more either. That was fine with me.

Then Lester and George heard me and Maggie

saying stuff like Stinky Potatoes and Gross Lizards, and they started, too. Then more kids began to say them and it got around. Maybe I was more of a genius than I thought.

That got me thinking that what I needed was a genius-type plan to make things at home more like they were at school. If I could get my dad back to the newspaper and my mom staying home, I'd be set. No more books, no more volleyball, just everything comfortable like it used to be, except I'd be a TV star. And I could tell about how I'd planned the whole thing. It would be great. Still, I didn't do anything about it until two days later. That night my dad said, "It looks like I might have to get an extension on the book."

"Does that mean you'll be home longer?" asked my mom.

"I'll have to be," he said.

"Fine with me," she said. "I'll be busy with report cards soon."

That was it. If I didn't do something right now, things might stay this way forever.

The next afternoon, Saturday, I went over to Maggie's. She was building a rocket model. I brought the puzzle I'd bought for Monica. When she threw it back at me I figured I might as well keep it, at least till I'd done it myself.

Maggie sat at the desk by her window, I spread out the puzzle on the floor, and we got busy. After a bit I said, "What are you going to do about

Russell?" Russell was still bugging Maggie about the tree house. "Well," said Maggie, "I haven't decided yet. I could dare him to bet me who gets the most points on TV and the winner gets the tree house, or I can tell him we'll never give him a chance to open his mouth unless he hands it over or—"

"But what if he won't bet you?" I said. "Or what if it snows first?"

Maggie looked up from her model. "Then there'd only be one thing to do, Cyril." She lowered her voice. "Sabotage."

"Sabotage?" I gulped.

"Ssh," said Maggie, "we can't talk about it now." She turned back to her work.

Wow, I thought, did she ever mean business. It was hard not to wish I was like her sometimes.

I started on the edges of the puzzle, and Maggie said, "Do you like having your dad home all the time?" She squinted at the retro rocket she was glueing. "I think it would be weird."

"Sure, I like it," I lied. How could I say I didn't want my own dad around the house? "What's so weird about it? He has to write his book someplace. Besides, your dad is home all day."

"That's different," Maggie said, "he's in the office and you can't just barge in and see him whenever you want. He's really busy."

"Well, so is my dad," I said. Maggie's dad wasn't going to be busier than mine. "And when he's not working he's thinking. We have to be quiet all the time and not disturb him. I practically never get to *talk* to him even, unless it's about his work. He asks me, you know." I fumbled with a puzzle piece that wouldn't quite fit. It was tough doing a puzzle on the carpet. "But when he's done, he'll maybe be famous. Rich, even."

"So? I barely even get to *see* my dad. He's got all these responsibilities now that we're a big family. My mom, too. I don't mind." Maggie sniffed. "I'm not a little baby anymore."

"Me either," I snorted. "Don't you hate it when they pat you on the head like a shrimpy little kindergartener?" Maggie bugged out her eyes and nodded. I said, "Doing things by yourself is loads better."

"Right," said Maggie. She dropped a model part by my foot. We nearly clunked heads reaching for it.

"Anyway," I tried to brag, "your mom is home all the time. Not like mine."

Maggie pushed her hair back behind her ears and picked up the glue. "She's got to be home, silly. She's looking after two babies, remember? She works even longer than my dad."

"Well, my mom is doing a volleyball tournament for eight whole schools and marking tests and she never even gets home till six-thirty!"

"Well, my mom says you don't know what work is till you have twins!" Maggie was almost shouting.

I yelled back, "Well, my mom —" and stopped. Down the hall the twins started bawling. Maggie and I glared at each other.

"Aw, who cares," I said, and shuffled the puzzle pieces. I didn't feel like arguing any more.

Maggie didn't say anything. She was bent low over the table, fiddling with the model, but when she reached to brush her hair back I saw her bottom lip was trembling.

I went home a little while later. The model and the puzzle got boring; we didn't feel like games or TV or talking. Trudging around the block to Greenapple Street, my boots ground on the hard packed snow. They made a sound like rabbits burping, but that didn't cheer me up. Nothing could, except my idea, and it was nowhere in sight.

I looked at the ice and snow piled high by the roadside and instead of climbing on it as usual, I thought about spring. It was a time for a change. I was tired of arguing and books and TV and busy grownups and bawling twins. I was tired of the whole thing.

Why couldn't things be the way they used to be when I was little? Little kids never had bad stuff happen to them like it happened to me. Or, if it did, someone came charging in and blubbering to them, like with the twins. Maggie's mother never went five feet away from them, even. I didn't want my mom taking me to the playground like I was a little shrimp or anything — I mean, I wasn't a *baby*. It was only with . . . that . . . had to . . .

"Incredible Gizzards!" I breathed, and took off for home. I had the telephone dialled before my jacket hit the floor. It wasn't going to be easy getting my parents to have a baby.

At first Maggie didn't want to do it. When I asked why she said never mind, and asked why I wanted to. I said never mind. We argued for a while but she finally gave in.

"Of course," she said, "you'll have to do anything—"

"No sweat," I said. I was so excited I didn't care if she made me dance around Room 7 in a ballerina suit.

"But, just remember," said Maggie, "if you're sorry later, don't blame me."

I guessed Maggie figured all babies were a pain, because of the twins. But this wasn't going to be twins. One baby was all I needed. I said, "Come over now," and hung up the phone. I was so excited I didn't mind when my dad made me put away my jacket. He won't be doing that much longer, I thought. I said, "Creepy Potatoes" and didn't care if he heard it.

As soon as Maggie came over we got to work. Our plan had four steps. I thought up the first two and Maggie got the last two. I thought hers were weird and she said mine were dumb, but I wanted to start right away.

First I had to get my parents thinking about babies, to soften them up, sort of. Maggie and I went to the basement and searched through the magazines and papers for baby stuff. Then I snuck upstairs and scattered them around the house. But my dad kept picking them up without looking at them. We watched him from inside the hall closet, so I know. He was on another planet, thinking about his book. He never noticed when I stuck my head into a bunch of coat hangers and they jangled all over. Maggie stuck her hand over my mouth so I didn't yell. It was going to be "Jerky Tomatoes."

"Told you," she sniffed, when we finally tumbled out.

"Wait till tomorrow," I said.

On Sunday morning I tried step two—telling my mom how neat the twins were any time she'd listen, which wasn't too often. She had school junk to do, and my Grampa was coming over for dinner. The twins weren't really neat, they were just small. All they did was lie around, cry and dribble, sleep, stuff like that.

"Useless, Cyril, useless," Maggie sighed when I called her. "We have to go to step three, *my first* step, right away."

"Can't we just skip it and go to step four?" I really hated step three.

"It's important," said Maggie, "and we made a deal. I'll be right over, or are you backing out?"

"Oooooooo, Hot Gizzards," I said. "No."

Step three was horrible, gross, and sickening. I

had to ask to see my own baby pictures. It did get my mom's attention, Maggie was right about that. Mom looked at me as if I had some weird disease, but she got the pictures and we all looked at them. My mom told Maggie embarrassing things about what a cute baby I was and I felt like a bozo.

"You didn't have to laugh *that* hard," I said when my mom left.

"I know Cyril, but, but . . ." Maggie tried to stop giggling.

"This is business," I said. "Anyway, I don't look that stupid, for a baby." I was getting a little tired of people laughing at me these days.

" . . . the one on the bearskin rug, I mean . . ." She broke up all over again. It didn't kill me when my dad, the Grumpy Tidier, barrelled in and put everything away ten minutes after we left the coffee table.

"Well, step three was more like it, huh?" said Maggie.

"Just get to step four," I said.

"Did you see how much your mom liked those pictures?" Maggie asked on Monday. "Right now she and your dad are thinking, 'Yup, sure was great having a baby.' "

"They haven't said anything to me," I grumbled. I was still grumpy about the baby pictures.

"Well, of course not," said Maggie. "They won't say it to you, but they'll think it, and that's what counts. So now we have to do the romantic dinner as soon as we can."

I liked the dinner idea. We were going to set it up for my parents and get me invited to Maggie's. Maggie said if we did it right my parents would get all mushy, like when they got married. And look what happened then—me.

"Thursday is the day," I said. "My dad's going out that afternoon so we can set up."

"Thursday! We could have wrapped this up a lot sooner if you had listened to me."

I groaned.

It took Tuesday and Wednesday to figure out what we'd need and to get me invited to Maggie's. On Thursday at lunch I asked my dad could I help with dinner because he was so busy. He was checking his briefcase for the fortieth time.

"We could come over and set the table and stuff for you before I go to Maggie's." I swept some crumbs off the table to show how helpful I was. They crackled under my feet as I stood up.

My dad said, "Well . . . yeah, all right! Thanks Cyril." He'd been more cheerful the last couple of days. Except for one meeting somewhere Tuesday morning, he'd stayed at his desk the whole time. That meant his book was going better, but he might turn back into the Grumpy Tidier any time. I was taking no chances.

My dad gave me the key I got to use sometimes and wrote down when to put the tuna casserole in the oven and how hot it was supposed to be.

"You're sure you want to do all this?" he asked.

"No sweat," I said.

"You're awfully interested in dinners all of a sudden."

The night before I'd asked a couple of questions about fancy dinners. Maggie told me what to say in case they got suspicious.

"It's for school. Like a project."

"This project I like," my dad said, snapping his briefcase shut. I sure hoped so.

Maggie and I got started right after school. It took nearly an hour but when we were done the dining room was ready for romance. We couldn't find a table-cloth so we used my bedspread. Except for the nubbly parts it looked just the same and the fringe looked nice. In the centre of the table we put a jug with these orange paper flowers my mom was saving for a garage sale. We had to bend them a little so you could see across the table. Then on either side we put candles, one tall green one and one short yellow one that kept mosquitoes away. I got the good knives and forks, some left-over Santa Claus napkins, and glasses for wine.

I got out the cardboard Cupid we'd put up at Valentine's and stuck it back up on the wall. Maggie found a record called *Heart Strings*, *Music for Lovers* by the Swinging Strings. Finally, we got the plastic bucket from under the sink, put ice in it and plunked this bottle of wine in it, also from under the sink. The label said Cooking Sherry, so we knew it was for dinner. Maggie put it by my dad's chair. Then I got the matches, lit the candles and turned off the dining-room light, while Maggie popped the casserole into the oven. Everything was ready. We stood in the doorway and checked it out. The sweet smell from the yellow candle floated over to us.

"It's good," Maggie nodded. "Not perfect, but close. You'll be glad I thought of this, Cyril. If you really like being a baby farmer, that is."

"A what?"

"A baby farmer. Like me, someone who looks after babies." I knew Maggie's mom looked after the babies, not Maggie. And that was just what my mom would do.

"I'll like it," I said.

"Okay," said Maggie, "but remember, I warned you."

"Uh-huh," I said, thinking *Oh yeah, sure.* "Hey, let's try the record." I put it on and flipped the switch. Violin music globbed out of the speakers. The smell of the mosquito candle and the oozy music made me feel like I was drowning in maple syrup. It was so disgusting we started to laugh. Then the record began to skip.

"Scratchy Gizzards!" I said.

"Forget it," Maggie said. "They'll be so busy looking deep into each other's eyes they'll never notice."

"Really?"

"Sure," said Maggie. "That's what happens on TV, right?"

"I guess," I said, but it made me nervous.

I turned off the stereo, and as the music disappeared we heard the rumble of the garage door.

"They're home!" I shouted.

"Hot Tomatoes!" said Maggie. "Let's get out of here."

The next three hours took forever. Maggie and I played a game, we fooled around with the twins for a while, we watched TV, but none of it helped.

"What do you think they're doing?" I whispered to Maggie. Maggie looked at her watch. "Probably they're eating dessert," she said.

"Eating dessert still?" I complained.

"Oh, Potato Gizzards, Cyril, you just asked two minutes ago."

"Well," I said, "I thought they might be doing the dishes."

"Are you kidding?" said Maggie. "They won't do those for a long time. Next they'll gaze deeper and deeper into each other's eyes and start babbling sweet nothings."

"Sweet what?" I asked.

"You know. Stuff like 'My beauteous desert flower' and 'My heart flutters like a captive butterfly' and 'Your eyes are dark and mysterious'." She wiggled her eyebrows and squinted at me.

"Where did you get this stuff?" I said. "It's disgusting."

Maggie flopped back on the couch. "I looked in some romance books. For research." She stretched out her arm. "And then, he'll take her hand, and *kiss* it madly." She smacked her way up her arm. I pretended to throw up. From the kitchen we heard Maggie's parents. They didn't sound very romantic; they were arguing. Maggie leaped up and flipped on the radio.

"Next," she said, over the music, "they'll dance." Before I knew it she'd yanked me out of my chair, spun me around the room, and snapped me so far backwards I felt like a pretzel. "And then," she looked down at me, "they'll *smooch*."

"Blecch!" I said, and she dropped me.

"Of course it's all completely yecchy," said Maggie, "but, *they* like it. Look," she pointed. On TV, two people were smooching.

"Gross," I said. "You'd think they'd hurt their noses."

"And your lips," said Maggie. "Think about your lips, too. Ugh," she shuddered, "that's pukey," and she changed the channel and turned off the radio.

Finally, at eight o'clock, I headed for home. As I zoomed up our walk, I looked for clues about what had happened. There was nothing. That made me more nervous. The porch light was on, the drapes were pulled across the living room window. I stopped at the door, took a deep breath, and pushed it open.

It was warm inside. Some old-guys-type record was playing on the stereo, the Beatles or somebody like that. I could just hear voices from the dining room. "Hi, Cyril," called my mom. "Come on in, honey."

I stepped over my coat and went through the living room. The dining room was dark. Only the green candle was burning, but I thought I could smell the yellow one a little. I could smell tuna casserole for sure. The stove light was on and I could see the dish sitting there. My parents were at the table, still dressed up from work — I mean my mom was, my dad was wearing his regular lumpy sweater. They were both smiling.

But were they romantic? It was hard to tell. With only one candle they probably couldn't even see each other's eyes, let alone stare deep into them.

"What's that?" I pointed at little glasses near their coffee cups.

"That's brandy," said my dad. "We're celebrating."

My heart jumped. "About what?"

My mom said, "Well, for one thing volleyball is over. And for another — well, your dad will tell you."

My Dad had a big grin on his face. "I don't want to tell you everything yet," he said, "just in case something goes wrong. But I'll give you a hint. I think a big problem got solved today and I might not get to hang around the house for as long as I thought. And you know what? You solved the problem. How do you like that?"

My heart was thumping like crazy. "Bald Potatoes," I breathed. They looked at each other and giggled as if they'd lost their brains. Romance was even weirder than I thought.

Then my mom said, "Well, pumpkin, this was just what we needed. Thanks a million." She reached out and gave me a big hug. My mind was racing so fast I didn't even squirm much. Before I could find out any more, they started asking me about my day and dinner at Maggie's. When I headed upstairs for my bath, I still wasn't absolutely, positively, cross-my-heart-and-hope-to-die sure I was going to be a baby farmer, but I would have bet you a million dollars.

Tall Potatoes

The last few days before the TV show I finally felt like the Greenapple Street Genius. My dad was pounding the typewriter all the time. Dishes piled up in the sink. He forgot to do the laundry. I skipped making my bed and he never even noticed. He was cheerful again, too. He kept humming this song over and over, and every so often he'd sing the words "baby face." Then one night through the heating vent, I heard him say something to my mom about "Small Potatoes." Their voices got lower after that. That had to be it. It was just like Maggie's parents. When Maggie's mom was going to have a baby they called it the Junior Partner, till they found out it was twins. Then they called them the Junior Partners. When I told Maggie all about "small potatoes" the next day, she wasn't sure, but she didn't know my parents like I did.

Now that I knew about it, a baby seemed neat.

It didn't have to be a pain. This one would definitely be a better baby. I could see me playing with it, showing it things. It would think I was really great, a genius older brother. I hinted a few times, but my parents pretended not to notice. That made me sure they were saving it as a surprise.

Things were great at school, too. People started saying I was funny. Everybody was saying things like "Hot Lizards" and "Heavy Tomatoes" all over the place. We were making up new ones every day. Monica was back to her old self, blabbing away all the time.

The only scary thing was the feud between Maggie and Russell. Russell kept pretending he was an angel to Mr. Flynn. But as soon as Mr. Flynn turned his back, Russell was sending notes to Maggie saying stuff like, "YOUR DUMP IS DOOMED," with a drawing of the tree house getting blown to smithereens. At first Maggie ignored them, but then she started making them into spitballs and paper airplanes and shooting them back. What if she got caught? Maybe Mr. Flynn would kick her off the TV team. Maybe Russell was even trying to make that happen. When I told her that, she just laughed.

"No way am I going to get caught throwing spitballs, Cyril. I'm the best." I guess she was too, but I was glad when she started sending Russell the weather forecasts from the morning paper instead. It looked like snow shovelling was over for this winter.

On Friday night the cold went away just like that and by Sunday there were bare patches on the lawns where the grass was all yellow and squashed. The snow banks along Greenapple Street melted down to black gunk. On Monday the first skipping ropes got brought to the school-yard. My boots started to feel like boulders chained to my feet. It was going to be time for runners soon.

"No snow, no money, no changing the tree house." Maggie gloated to me Monday morning. "It's TV on Wednesday. Tomorrow I'm going to nail that despicable little rodent. I'll tell him we'll fry him on TV if I don't get the tree house back." She laughed on purpose like a mad scientist in a monster movie. "Fiendish Lizards."

"Are you sure it will work?" I said. "You better be careful, 'cause Mr. Flynn says we're supposed to be a team, remember."

"Cyril!" said Maggie. "Dumb Potatoes, what's more important, some stupid team with Monica and Russell or my tree house?"

Before I could answer somebody yelled to her and she took off. That was good, because all I knew was TV was too important to mess up. I didn't want to be a mushmouth again.

It was getting harder and harder for me to pay attention. Mr. Flynn asked me to be quiet three times, but I just couldn't. Monica talked a mile a minute too. Maggie and Russell soaked themselves and about fifty others in a splashing contest in one of the big puddles at recess. Russell even got in trouble for drawing monsters instead of colouring in his map and Maggie finally got caught shooting a spitball.

Mr. Flynn asked the four of us to stay behind for a few minutes. He said he was counting on us to set a good example in the next couple of days and he knew we were responsible enough to do that, weren't we. We all said yes, sir. Then he reminded us about team work and told us not to worry and asked were we concerned about anything. Monica asked should we get dressed up for Wednesday. Mr. Flynn said neatness was what counted. We couldn't think of anything else, so he let us go.

We went down the hall arguing about getting dressed up. Monica wanted to, Russell didn't, Maggie said do what you want, and I didn't know. I usually hate dressing up, but maybe you were supposed to for TV. When we reached the doors Russell took off with Bobby, Monica called to Karina, and nothing got decided.

"Do you think Mr. Flynn wants us to dress up?" I asked Maggie as we started along the schoolyard.

"Stinky Tomatoes, Cyril, he doesn't care. He just kept us in to tell us to behave ourselves. And

I don't care either. Know what I'm doing tonight?" She slid her boots happily through the mud. "I'm going out for pizza with my mom. Just the two of us. Then we're going to the library the way we used to."

We waded slowly through the middle of puddles like giants walking in lakes. Maggie talked about pizza and I listened to the squishes and gurgles from the puddles and wondered if I'd hear anything more about Small Potatoes tonight. We split up by the bicycle racks and I hurried up Greenapple Street. The sun had gone behind a long dark cloud. Spring or not, it was cold.

It must have started in the middle of the night because when I woke up the next morning the whole world was grey and white and the snow was still swirling down. Maggie won't like this, I thought. But maybe getting fried on TV would still scare Russell off anyways.

"You know what they say about March," my dad said when I went down for breakfast. "In like a lion, out like a lamb." Still, it didn't seem right that it should snow now. It just wasn't fair.

My mom stood up as I sat down, but her sweater was too bulky to see if she was any bigger yet. Then I had my first genius-type idea of the day. "I wish we could tape my show," I said, " 'cause probably some people won't be able to see it who'll want to."

"Mmm-hmm, well, we'll see, pumpkin," said my mom, looking into the fridge.

I went on carefully, "So like, if Grampa is busy or we forget to watch, or," I made it sound like it just popped into my head, "or somebody was too *little* to see it . . . "

I crossed my toes, waiting.

But my dad just said, "Somebody too little?"

I fidgeted in my chair but there was no backing out now. Playing with my spoon, I said, "I don't know, say there was a baby or something."

"Well, you don't have to worry about that." My mom closed the fridge. "There's not going to be any babies around here."

At first it was like the words got stuck in my ears and couldn't get into my brain. Then it was like a snowpile whomping on me. "Aren't—you're not—not going—"

"To have a baby? Of course not, dear." My mom smiled. "Why ever would you think that?"

"But you—when I came home—you were celebrating. Dad sang Baby Face! You said—" I felt as if the room was spinning.

"Oh gosh, Cyril, no," said my dad, "we were celebrating my book, that the problem got solved. I just hummed that song for something happy."

"I wondered why you kept talking about babies," said my mom. "But sweetie, you don't have to worry. You're enough for us, remember? From now on the only babies born around here will be your father's books." She mussed my hair, then kissed me. "Now I've got to scoot. This darn storm is going to make me late."

A half hour later I was stomping down the street myself. How could they get it all backwards? How could *I* get it all backwards? I whaled a snowball at the mail box and missed. It was all because of that stupid book. I reached for more snow, then froze. My mother had said BOOKS! MORE OF THEM? I groaned and let the snow slip from my mittens. "Crummy Potatoes," I sighed, and pushed on for school.

When I got there, Mr. Flynn was waiting for me. He told me to go to the library right away.

Maggie and Russell and Monica were already there. Monica was blabbing to no one in particular about a horse book. Maggie was flopped on the comfy couch looking at a science book. She had a big smile on her face. Russell was staring out at the snow. He looked kind of stunned. Maggie had probably just threatened to fry him, but I didn't much care.

Mr. Flynn strode in and took us to a table in the far corner. He seemed angry, sort of, and I got a little nervous. Was he mad at us? I looked fast at Maggie. She shrugged.

Mr. Flynn gave his moustache one brush and sighed. "You people have done a wonderful job on this TV project," he said, "and I'm proud of you. I hope you're proud of yourselves, too. You really came through on this one and I want to thank you."

It was nice and all, but I wasn't really in the

mood. I wished Mr. Flynn would just say whatever he had to say.

He went on, "Unfortunately, not everyone has come through on this as well as you did. We have a problem."

My head snapped up like an elastic band. The elevator started running in my stomach. Mr. Flynn sighed. "After you left yesterday, I got a call from the TV people. They were very embarrassed and very sorry, but they said that a mistake had been made."

The elevator in my stomach rode to my throat. I held on tight to my chair.

"Somehow they invited too many schools for this season's shows and they had to tell us we couldn't come tomorrow, that we'd be on next year instead. Next year all of you will be in the wrong grade, so we're not going to be on TV."

The elevator dropped about 800 stories and everything smashed into a million pieces. Mr. Flynn was sorry. So what? We'd get Challengers T-shirts anyway, big deal. Kids stared from the classrooms as we walked back through the empty halls. I couldn't have cared less. I found my seat and that was the last attention I paid. Current events didn't matter. Social studies was stupid junk. I just stared out the window at the falling snow. Recess went by, library. I didn't even care when the principal announced that school was closing at noon because of the snow and that if you went home for lunch you should stay there.

Nothing really came through till I was pulling on my boots outside Room 7 and I heard Russell talking to Bobby and two kids from another class. "I don't care," he said. "My dad knows the weather man at the TV station. I can go any time I want. Besides, we might've lost anyway. The team wasn't exactly all brainers, eh?"

The other three snickered. Suddenly I was so mad I couldn't talk. But another voice said, "Oh Russell, shut up. You think you're so smart! We would have been a good team, so there!" and Monica was glaring from the doorway.

"Yeah, Russell," I croaked, "so who asked you, anyway!"

Russell turned to look at us.

"Aw, why don't you two go get married," he said. Bobby and the others howled.

Monica looked him straight in the eye. "Russell, you're a dwork." She turned on her heel and marched up the hall. "Right," I yelled, and hurried after her. Behind us Bobby called, "Bye-bye, Rubbernose! Bye, Blubbermouth! Happy honeymoon!" Russell yelled, "Tell Maggie I'll clean off her driveway right after lunch." We didn't look back. They were still laughing when we turned our different ways at the doors.

"Bye, Cyril," said Monica.

"Bye, Monica," I said, and headed out into the snow storm. I pushed across the school yard, boiling mad at nearly everything.

I didn't slow down until I ran into Maggie. She was shuffling head down past the deserted bike racks. The long trenches in the snow behind her feet were filling up. She didn't answer when I spoke, or even look at me when I told her about Russell.

"What are you so sad about," I snapped. "You'll get your tree house somehow. You're still the Maple Avenue Marvel. Nobody calls you Rubbernose."

"So what are you so sad about," she snapped right back. "You don't have to be a genius. And nobody cares if I am, anyway. I'm just expected to be. You'll go home and everybody will go, 'Oooh, poor baby,' 'cause you're the only one. Your dad will probably write a book about you or something." She swatted at a bush with her mitten.

I exploded. "He will not! He probably won't even want me home, he's so busy with his dumb book. That's all they talk about. And what are you so sad about? I thought you liked it busy at your house, and your mom takes you for pizza and to the library."

"*So what are you so sad about*!" Maggie yelled, "*You'll* be rich and famous and your mom and dad will be home all the time. And for your information *I hate it* since I moved 'cause my dad's always busy and my mom's looking after the stupid twins. And she didn't take me for pizza OR library and I might as well be dead!"

85

"Yeah?" I screeched. "Well, FOR YOUR INFORMATION we will not be rich, we will not be famous, I hate his stupid book and I hate it when he stays home because he fusses all the time and my mom stays at school and I might as well be dead, too. And they're not having a baby either, so there. My parents are DUMB!"

"Well so are mine!" Maggie screamed.

We stared at each other. I felt like I'd just yelled swear words in Sunday School. It was as if the words were still there and they wouldn't go away.

Maggie said softly, "I didn't really mean all that, exactly. I guess I'm just mad about TV."

"Me too." We started to walk. I started to breathe again.

Maggie said, "Did you want a baby so your mom would stay home and your dad go out?"

I nodded. "But they're not going to."

"That's too bad," said Maggie. "But believe me, Cyril, you wouldn't have liked it."

"Maybe," I said, "but I was just so sure." Then I remembered. "You weren't, though. How'd you know?"

"Oh, I don't know," said Maggie. I didn't believe her.

"C'mon," I said. Finding out was better than wondering how dumb I'd been.

"Well," Maggie said like she was apologizing, "it was the 'Small Potatoes' stuff. I found it in the dictionary. It means something not important. We call the twins the Junior Partners, but partner says they're important. *We're* the small potatoes, Cyril."

I sighed. There didn't seem to be much else that could go wrong today.

My dad had lunch ready when I got home. He listened all the way through as I told him about TV, and Russell, too. It didn't seem to bug him that I'd be home all afternoon. In fact, he never mentioned his book once till lunch was done. Then he said, "Come on in the den."

From the folder on his desk he took out two pieces of paper.

"Take a look," he said. "One is the dedication page and the other is for the title page. I've been saving these as a surprise, but I think now is the right time."

I looked. The first paper said:

This book is to JAN, my wife, for much help and understanding, and to CYRIL, who gave me the key to the whole thing. Thanks a million.

"Huh?" I looked at my dad.
"Read the title," he said.
I fumbled with the other sheet:

SMALL POTATOES, HOT TOMATOES:
Entrepreneurs and the New Marketplace

"I heard you saying Hot Tomatoes and Lizards Gizzards and all that when I was stumped for a new way to organize the book. It got me thinking, so I went back to see the man who said them to me. We talked some more and I worked out my idea. Instead of talking about businesses one at a time, I've put them in groups. Some are Lizzard's Gizzards, some are Small Potatoes, some are Hot Tomatoes. It all depends on whether they're bad ideas, little things that won't earn much, or really hot deals, you see?" He laughed. "It was something about the way you used the words. They just seemed so catchy when I heard them again. I really liked how you changed 'small potatoes' to '*bald* potatoes'. I wish I could have used it. Anyway, the publishers loved it. The whole book is worked out thanks to you, and I've got an idea for another one, all about this same man. I hope you can suffer through it with me. I'll need help."

Well. I couldn't tell my dad he wasn't supposed to have heard me. I couldn't tell him that bald potatoes started out as a mistake, that I'd heard wrong. I didn't know how to tell him he made me feel not so dumb. So, I said, "Sure. Thanks," instead.

"Thank *you*," he said back. "It's not TV, but it's yours."

"Can I show it to people?" I asked.

"You can tell them, if you want, and show them as soon as the book gets printed."

I closed the door softly as I left, so as not to disturb my dad. He needed quiet for working on a great book. I needed quiet to look out the window and feel happy.

It stopped snowing about three o'clock. Tobogganing, I thought, or snow forts. It would be excellent packing snow. Then Maggie called and said, "Snow shovelling." I groaned.

"Aw, not again," I said. "What for? You know Russell's gonna clean us."

"Cyruullll," Maggie said, "I have a plan. In fact, I've got two. Now come on. Don't forget, you owe me for baby farming."

"But—"

"We've gotta hurry," said Maggie. "See you at Elstons'," and she hung up.

I said, "Snowball Potato Gizzards" and went for my coat.

When I got to Elstons' Maggie was doing the driveway. I started the walk. She didn't seem nearly as sad as before. She had her old I've-got-a-secret smile on. No matter how much I bugged her she wouldn't tell me what her plans were, so I asked her something else instead. "Hey Maggie, did you really mean that stuff we said while we were coming home?"

Maggie grunted and heaved a shovelful of snow. "Well, some," she said. "Now my mom says we'll go out tonight instead and my dad says I don't have to phone the office before I come to visit if it's really big news."

"So it's all better," I said.

"No," she said, "but it's okay." She turned right around to me. "Did you mean what you said?"

"Kind of," I admitted, and told her about the book. I left out the part about Bald Potatoes being Small Potatoes, though. That made me seem a little smarter. "Now my dad says he has an idea for another book. It's pretty tough living with a writer, you know. But I guess I can handle it. Anyway, at least we're not the small potatoes."

Maggie nodded, and then I said, "Look!" Russell was coming down the street, dragging his snow thrower. "It's about time," said Maggie. "Start shovelling."

I kept my head down—I'd had enough of Russell for one day—but Maggie called, "Hey, Russell!" as he came by.

I heard Russell stop and laugh. "Why don't you two just pack it in? I'll finish the street." I kept shovelling, but inside I was groaning.

"Talk, talk, talk, Russell," Maggie said. "You can't even do Old Man Billings' place. But I guess you heard he pays rotten and gives the most work."

I stopped shovelling and stared at Maggie as if she was out of her mind. Russell laughed again.

"Nice try," he said. "I'm not that dumb. Cyril said last time it was the best job on the street. So I'll go get it right now while you're stuck here.

Thanks for reminding me, turkey. Kiss your tree house bye-bye."

"Oh, you'll get it all right," said Maggie, watching him run back down the street, his snow thrower bumping behind him. "*I* think he's that dumb. Do you think he's that dumb, Cyril?"

Before I could answer, Maggie said, "Way to set him up for it, Cyril, telling him how good it was last time. I knew we were thinking of the same trick." Maggie laughed. "I wonder if you can use a snow thrower on a gravel driveway?"

We watched as Russell talked to Old Man Billings, then started up the snow thrower. For a few seconds it went REEEEEEE, then it made a noise like turkeys in a washing machine and stones were shooting off Old Man Billings' house. Old Man Billings stuck his head out the door and started yelling and Russell stopped the snow thrower. You could see him keep nodding his head as Old Man Billings jabbered and waved his arms. The door closed and Russell trudged back of the house. He came back carrying a shovel.

"Gee," Maggie said as he set to work, "too bad the snow is so heavy." She turned back to her work. "Well, on to plan number two."

"Number two?" I asked cautiously.

"Simple, Cyril. Starting with the fortune I make this afternoon, I'm going to save up and buy my own tree-house kit. I don't care what he does with the old one. It's time for a change."

"There's no room in your back yard," I said.

"Well, what about your place?" Maggie asked.

"*Yeah*," I said, "we can share it. I'll help. Let's make it big!"

"Right. Big enough so we can have other people in it, too."

"Like George."

"And Tracy."

"And Monica."

When we finished naming everybody we'd invite Maggie said, "Not bad for small potatoes, huh, Cyril?"

"Ha!" I said. "We're not small potatoes, we're . . . we're Tall Potatoes!"

"All *right*!" said Maggie. We slapped mittens and went back to work. The Tall Potatoes were digging out towards Spring.

More Good Books

Maggie and Me
Ted Staunton

Poor Cyril! Without Maggie life would be a lot easier,
but it would also be a lot more boring. MAGGIE
AND ME — a collection of five funny stories starring
Cyril and his best friend Maggie, the Greenapple Street
Genius. No matter what they do, they seem to be in
trouble.

Ted Staunton wanted to be a cowboy when he was
small, but somehow he became a writer instead. He is
also a musician and will perform his songs for anyone
who wants to listen. The author of *Puddleman*, *Taking
Care of Crumley* (also starring Cyril and Maggie) and
Simon's Surprise, he is married and lives in Toronto.

Kids Can Press